MY 1ST GRAPHIC NOVEL

AIRPLANE ADVENTURE

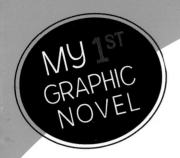

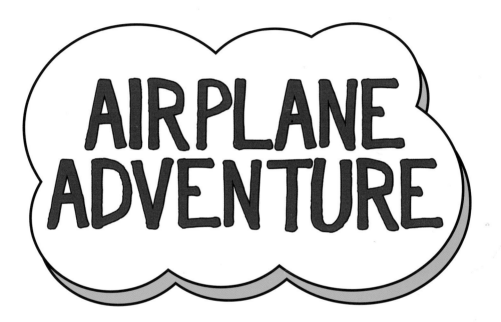

My First Graphic Novels are published by Stone Arch Books
151 Good Counsel Drive, P.O. Box 669
Mankato, Minnesota 56002
www.stonearchbooks.com

Library of Congress Cataloging-in-Publication Data
Meister, Cari.
    Airplane adventure / by Cari Meister ; illustrated by Marilyn Janovitz.
    p. cm. — (My first graphic novel)
    ISBN 978-1-4342-1618-2 (library binding)
    1. Graphic novels. [1. Graphic novels. 2. Air travel—Fiction. 3. Airplanes—Fiction.
4. Mexican Americans—Fiction.] I. Janovitz, Marilyn, ill. II. Title.
PZ7.7.M45Ai 2010
741.5'973—dc22

                                        2008053375

Summary: Juan and Anna take a trip on an airplane to visit their grandma in Mexico.

Creative Director: Heather Kindseth
Graphic Designer: Emily Harris

AIRPLANE ADVENTURE

by Cari Meister

illustrated by
Marilyn Janovitz

STONE ARCH BOOKS
MINNEAPOLIS   SAN DIEGO

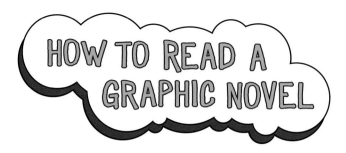

HOW TO READ A GRAPHIC NOVEL

Graphic novels are easy to read. Boxes called panels show you how to follow the story. Look at the panels from left to right and top to bottom.

Read the word boxes and word balloons from left to right as well. Don't forget the sound and action words in the pictures.

The pictures and the words work together to tell the whole story.

Juan and Anna are going to Mexico.
They are going to see their grandma.

It is too far to walk.
It is too far to drive.

They will fly on an airplane.

Juan packs his flippers and snorkel for the beach.

Anna packs her book about shells.

They pack some treats
for the plane ride too.

ZIP ZIP ZIP

The airport is busy.

Anna and Juan get their tickets.

They give their bags to the ticket taker.

They hug their dad good-bye.

They go to the security area.

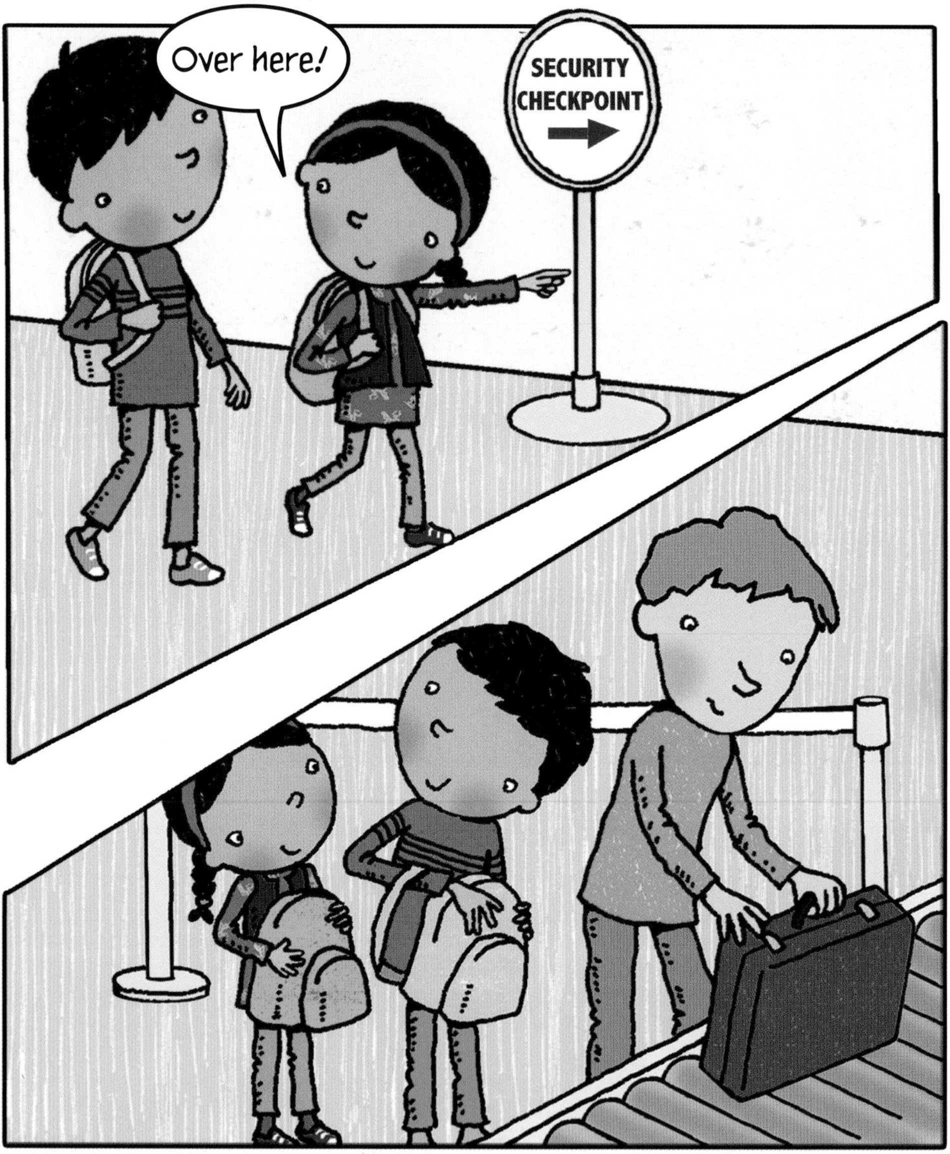
Over here!
SECURITY
CHECKPOINT

Juan and Anna put their backpacks on a moving belt.

A camera looks inside their backpacks.

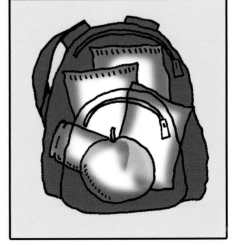

Anna takes off her shoes. She walks through the metal frame.

Juan takes off his shoes too. Then he walks through the metal frame.

He empties his pockets.

Now he does not beep.

An airport worker shows them where to wait.

Soon it is time to board the airplane.

Anna and Juan find their seats.

The captain talks to the passengers over the loudspeaker.

The flight attendant tells them the safety rules.

The plane starts to move slowly.
Then it goes faster and faster.

Juan feels a little scared.

In the air, everything looks small.

Anna uses the bathroom.

They watch a movie.

The captain's voice comes
over the loudspeaker again.

The wheels come out.
The plane gets louder.

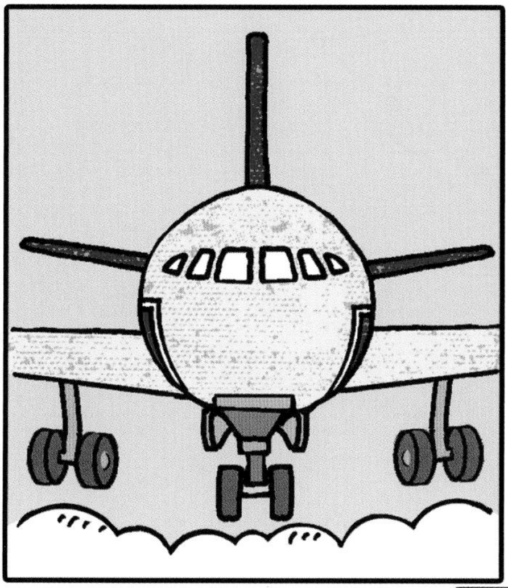

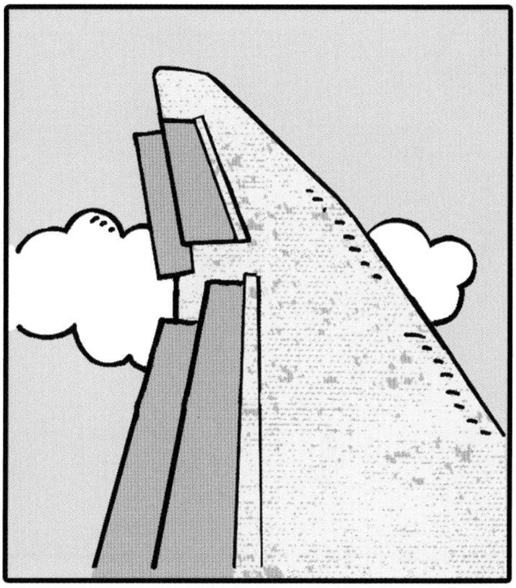

The wing flaps lift.

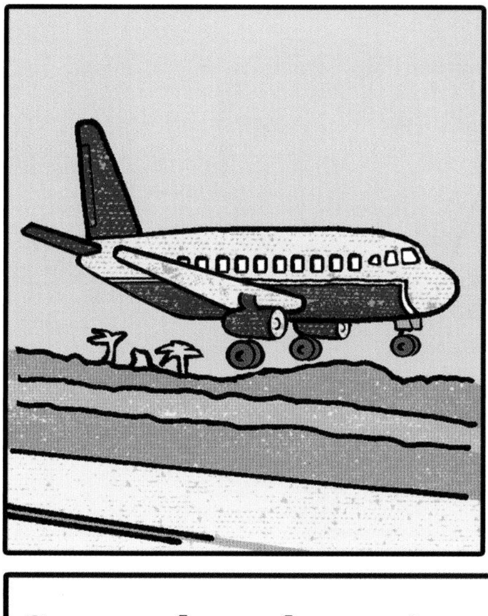

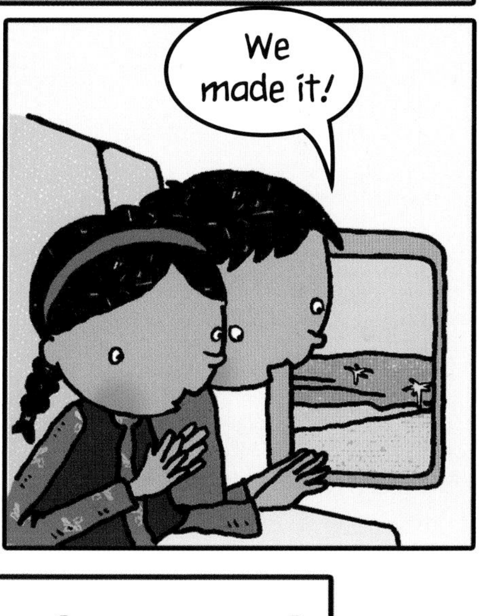
We made it!

Soon the plane is on the ground.

Anna and Juan get off the airplane.

What a fun trip!

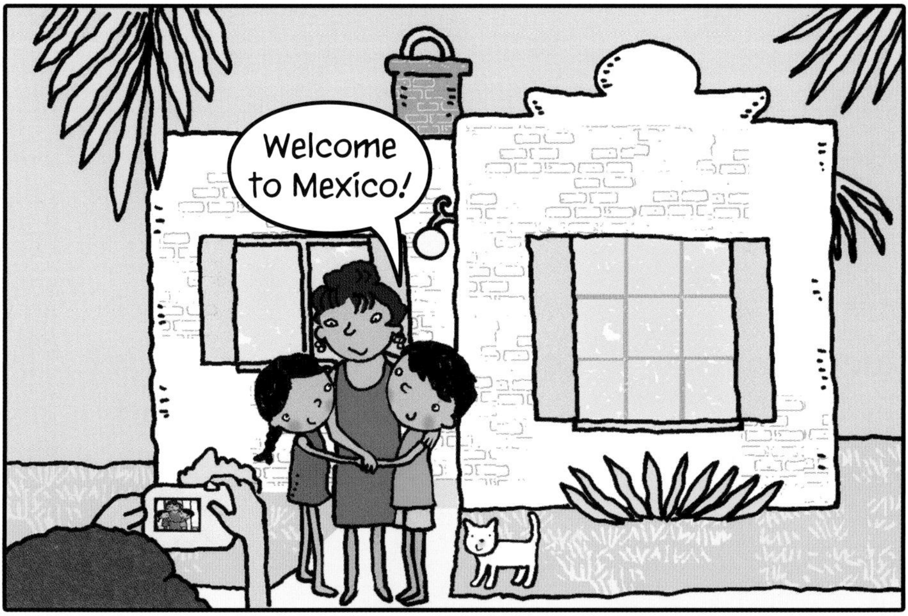
Welcome to Mexico!

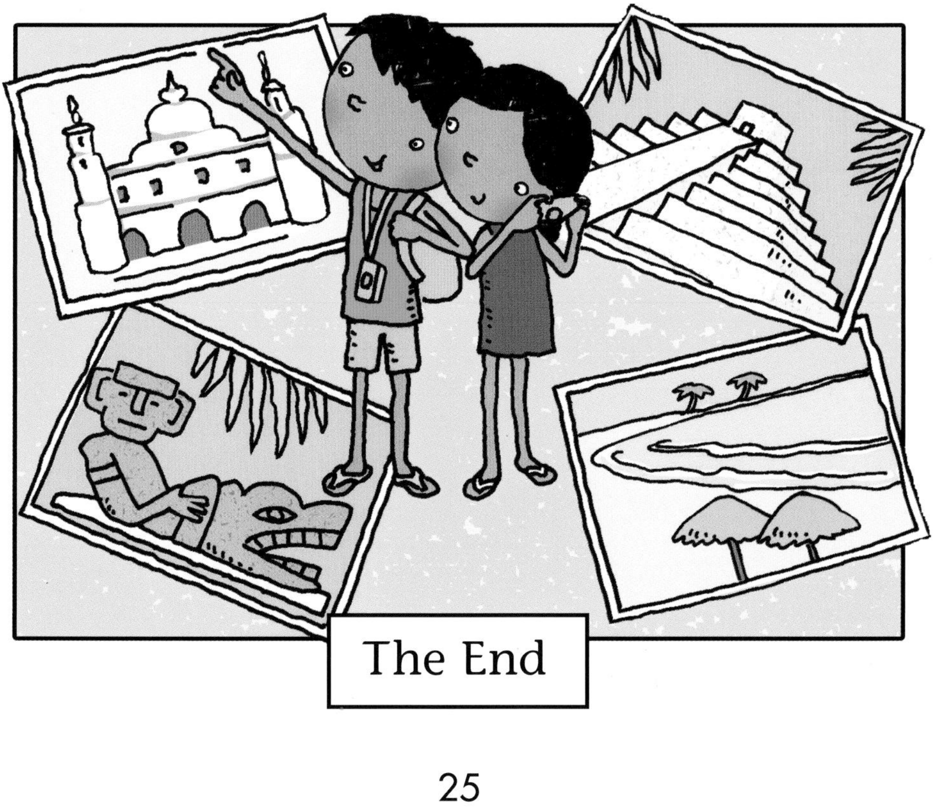

The End

ABOUT THE AUTHOR

Cari Meister is the author of many books for children, including the My Pony Jack series and *Luther's Halloween*. She lives on a small farm in Minnesota with her husband, four sons, three horses, one dog, and one cat. Cari enjoys running, snowshoeing, horseback riding, and yoga. She loves to visit libraries and schools.

ABOUT THE ILLUSTRATOR

Marilyn Janovitz has written and illustrated numerous books for children. Many of her books have been translated into several languages. Marilyn's work has also been used in advertising, editorial, and textile design. Marilyn works in her closet-sized studio, where she can look out and see the Empire State Building twenty blocks away.

GLOSSARY

airport (AIR-port)—a place where planes take off and land

attendant (uh-TEN-duhnt)—someone who looks after a person or object

board (BORD)—to get on

loudspeaker (LOUD-spee-kur)—a machine that makes a voice louder

security area (si-KYOOR-uh-tee AIR-ee-uh)—a place that is closely watched so people stay safe

DISCUSSION QUESTIONS

1.) Juan gets scared on the airplane. Have you ever been scared about something? What was it?

2.) Anna and Juan pack some things for their trip. Have you ever been on a trip? Where did you go? What did you pack?

3.) Would you like to go on an airplane? Why or why not?

WRITING PROMPTS

1.) If you could go anywhere in the world, where would you go? Draw a picture of that place.

2.) Draw a picture of your own airplane. Be sure to include a name on the plane.

3.) Throughout the book, there are sound and action words next to some of the picture. Pick at least two of those words. Then write your own sentences using those words.

THE 1ST STEP INTO GRAPHIC NOVELS

These books are the perfect introduction to graphic novels. Combine an entertaining story with comic book panels, exciting action elements, and bright colors, and a safe graphic novel is born.

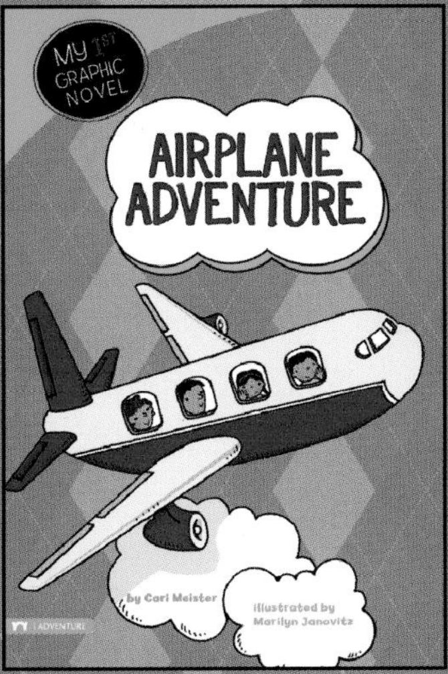
MY 1ST GRAPHIC NOVEL
AIRPLANE ADVENTURE
by Cari Meister
illustrated by Marilyn Janovitz
ADVENTURE

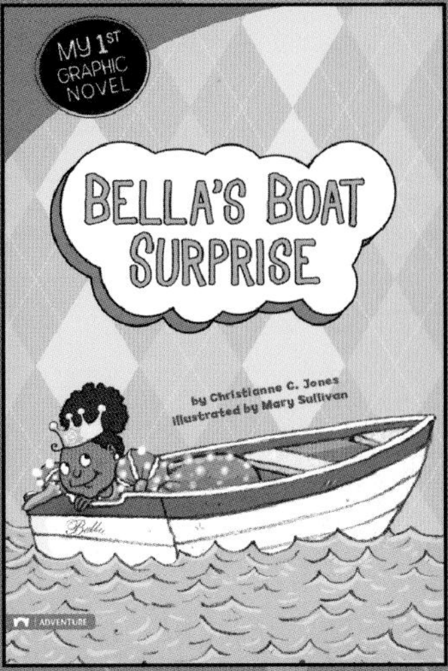
MY 1ST GRAPHIC NOVEL
BELLA'S BOAT SURPRISE
by Christianne C. Jones
illustrated by Mary Sullivan
ADVENTURE

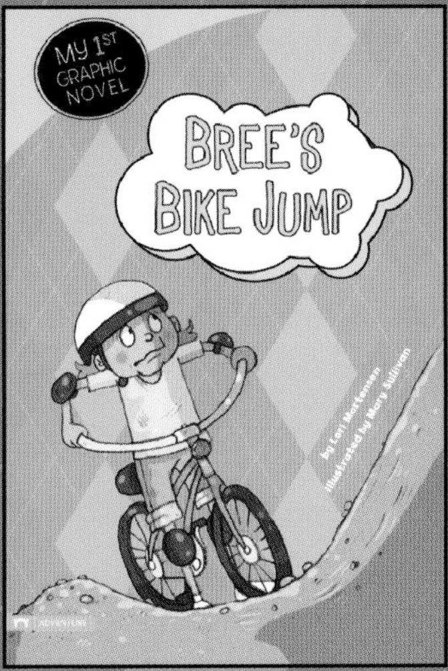
MY 1ST GRAPHIC NOVEL
BREE'S BIKE JUMP
by Lori Mortensen
illustrated by Mary Sullivan
ADVENTURE

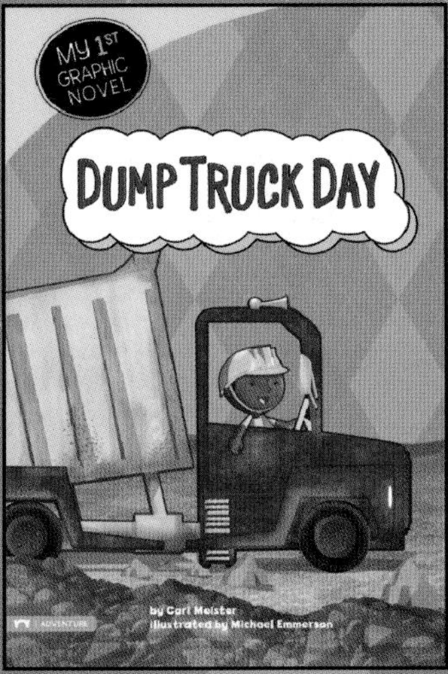
MY 1ST GRAPHIC NOVEL
DUMP TRUCK DAY
by Cari Meister
illustrated by Michael Emmerson
ADVENTURE

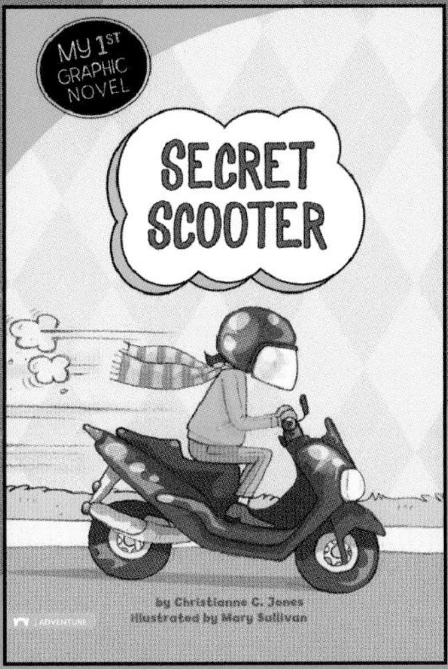
MY 1ST GRAPHIC NOVEL
SECRET SCOOTER
by Christianne C. Jones
illustrated by Mary Sullivan
ADVENTURE

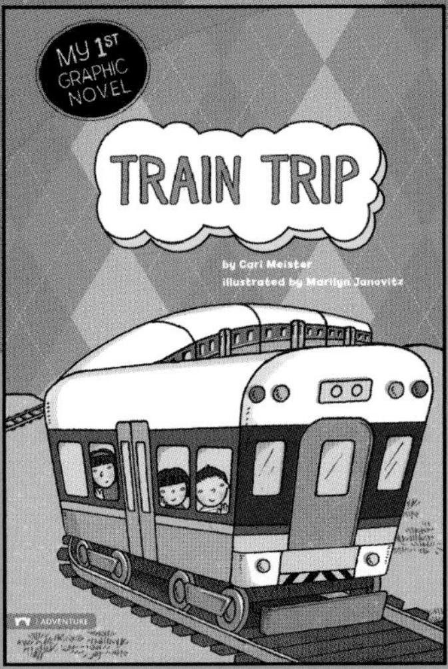
MY 1ST GRAPHIC NOVEL
TRAIN TRIP
by Cari Meister
illustrated by Marilyn Janovitz
ADVENTURE